About the Author

"I've always loved writing poems since I was a child, mostly funny limericks but a few heartbreakers when life wasn't going so well.

I won a number of Medical Society limerick competitions under the pseudonym of Fido or Bart Simpson!

I wrote for family and friends and gradually the word has spread."

Kate Condon

For my father, Tom Scott, who introduced and emphasised the importance of doggerel and LOVE to lift one's spirits.

Kate Condon

LIMERICKS FOR EVERY OCCASION

AUSTIN MACAULEY
PUBLISHERS LTD.

Copyright © Kate Condon (2016)

The right of Kate Condon to be identified as author of this work has been asserted by her in accordance with section 77 and 78 of the Copyright, Designs and Patents Act 1988.

All rights reserved. No part of this publication may be reproduced, stored in a retrieval system, or transmitted in any form or by any means, electronic, mechanical, photocopying, recording, or otherwise, without the prior permission of the publishers.

Any person who commits any unauthorized act in relation to this publication may be liable to criminal prosecution and civil claims for damages.

A CIP catalogue record for this title is available from the British Library.

ISBN 9781785540110 (Paperback)
ISBN 9781785540127 (Hardback)
ISBN 9781785540134 (eBook)

www.austinmacauley.com

First Published (2016)
Austin Macauley Publishers Ltd.
25 Canada Square
Canary Wharf
London
E14 5LQ

Printed and bound in Great Britain

Thanks to James Condliffe of 3DJAC for his delightful illustrations!

Contents

Impossible Rhymes 2
People 4
Animals 10
Birthday 16
Bridesmaids 20
Best Man 24
Get Well 28
Mother's Day & Father's Day 32
New Home 36
New Year 40
New Baby 44
New Job 48
Sad 50
Thanks 54
Engagement 58
Valentine 60
Exams 62
Retirement 66
Random 70

Impossible Rhymes

Orange has nothing with which to rhyme
The angst this has given me's a crime
Silver's quite sticky
Purple's quite tricky
Maybe I'll write one this week some time...

I'm Mary, I've a little lamb
Don't know if it's a girl, oh damn!
I paid the vet silver
He said; "It's a chilver!"
Shall I call it Dolly or Pam?

Did Buddha die from mouldy curry?
His monks wear robes, walk slow, not hurry
(They're saffron, not orange)
Was it death mould sporange?
Avyaakata, so no worry...

On Prince Philip's day, Kate wore purple
Now 90s, he has a slight hirple
No longer on boats
Says non PC quotes
Such as "horses a**," or "you curple"

People

There was a young man from Peru
Who sprinted to Machu Picchu
He is fit, full of beans
Only just in his teens
His secret is alpaca stew

There once was a student from Leeds
Who grew in his garden some weeds
He smoked what he grew
Put some in his stew
And then went to jail for bad deeds

A handsome young man from Peru
Spent most of his life in a zoo
He's fit, full of beans
And just in his teens
Then married a lady Gnu

There is a young man lives in Leeds
Who spends his days doing good deeds
He hates HS2
"Won't benefit you!
Long countrywide freight trains - yes please..."

I know a thin man who is old
In winter he goes blue with cold
In fact he's my dad
And I'm very glad
He loves me - "more precious than gold."

There is a man living in Dorset
Wears smart suits and 'neath them a corset
Fat tummy is round
Eats cheese by the pound
His man girdle - he has to force it

I know a tall girl with twelve toes
They wiggle wherever she goes
"My balance is better"
She said when I met her
Then tripped and fell flat on her nose

There's a man living in Crawley
Ate doughnuts 'til he was poorly
And he will quite soon
Burst like a balloon
Think moderation's best surely

A Portsmouth lady went for a run
It wasn't a race, but just for fun
She hadn't gone far
Got hit by a car
Now runs in heaven towards the sun…

A garrulous lady from here
Who daily drinks ten pints of beer
She says it's the hops
Gives bad windy pops
"My friends have all left me, I fear!"

A woman who wears black and white
Shirt and trousers, always too tight
She walks many miles
Chats nonstop and smiles
Like zebras but not quite as bright

There was an old man came from Truro
Banged his head and turned up in Neuro
Confused and fuzzee
He thought it was free
But they charged him ten thousand Euro

I'd love to meet the Dalai Lama
His smiling eyes make me feel calmer
Less suffering/desire
Let's aim a bit higher
More joy and peace - less harmful drama!

Animals

In Oklahoma, the armadillo
Dead on the road, blows up like a pillow
Like hedgehogs in Britain
There's thousands get smitten
By fast cars, so chill, be kind and drive slow...

Jess's cat Nutty should be called Natty
Eats too much food and now is a fatty
She's so soft and pretty
A delightful kitty
Her parents smitten, mad and quite batty

I know a cute dog with a brain
Who writes verses with a refrain
His chorus is clever
Great canine endeavour
His poems - true dogg'rel, INSANE!

See tee shirts: "Keep calm and carry on"
Watch Match of The Day - see Gary on
Do animals too
Talk like me and you?
See vultures wait, then eat carrion...

There was an old man from Bilbao
Whose pussycat couldn't miaow
In her early life
She chewed a sharp knife
Since that time she lisps a bow-wow!

The best dog alive is called Sadie
Kind, funny, a beautiful lady
Smiles, then mystifies
With big soulful eyes
When sunny she sits where it's shady

There was a Komodo dragon
Who drank red wine from a flagon
His rapping at school
Considered quite cool
With hoody and trousers saggin'

A hornet's a big wasp times ten
If trapped, calls his mate and brethren
A million will come
Sting face, arms (and bum)!
So spare it - or squish it right then...

My old horse plays the didgeridoo
He has just joined the orchestra too
My dog plays the drums
All fingers and thumbs
Conductor is Captain Kangaroo...

I'm in love with Alfie the dog
Dream of when we went for a jog
We ran hills so steep
Ten miles, chased a sheep
But sadly he's not mine to hog...

There's no such thing as a 'rogue' shark
They're hunting lunch, not for a lark
You look like a seal
Have surfboard appeal
In the wrong place? Your future's stark!

Young Finn is the best horse, it's true
Connemara, dun 15-2
The baby of Fran
Together they can
Learn eventing - show jumping too

I do think prairie dogs are cute
They eat green grass and bugs and root
Run tunnels all day
New Mexico way
Make comical squeaks- they're not mute

Many species nature's accrued
Pollinate much fruit and veg food
Most US bees - tiny
They won't sting your heinie
Soon they'll be gone, then we'll be screwed!

Birthday

Birthday

Dear Emma you're fifty years old
And worried you'll soon turn to mould
If you were a cat
You're seven times that
Don't worry, get happy, be bold!

Fourteen is a wonderful year
Be crazy, go wild, have no fear
Your parents complain
Again and again
Don't worry, they're still glad you're here

Ten years old and growing so fast
Your baby years, they didn't last
You're pretty and clever
I'll love you forever
Happy birthday, go have a blast

So Kerry, you're 60 today
You've come up to London to play
A trip with no worry
Which ends with a curry
And fam'ly sings Happy Birthday

Wonderful day to be thirty
Still cute and clever yet flirty
So come out with me
I'll order some tea
I'll pay, so you won't get shirty!

An old bag from Portreath - (that's me)
Her birthday she swam out to sea
Kate at fifty seems
Fulfilled long term dreams
Swam Gull Rock and back home - Yippee!

Happy Birthday little bro'
Forty nine, an old man - NO
George is his name
Crazy's his game
BFG I love you so...

Bilbo Baggins is eleventy-one
His birthday had dragons - looked good fun
He then disappeared
Which looked rather weird
Nine hours later, the trilogy's done

Woke up this morning feeling great
Jo-Jo's birthday, mustn't be late
A poem I wrote
And twenty pound note
Eat lots of cake - bet you can't wait

Bridesmaids

What a great time, but quite a shock
Out all night until five o'clock
Danced, drank through the town
Danced more and fell down
Best hen party, my bridesmaids rock

The bridesmaids look gorgeous in blue
With the bride, it's a stunning view
Each shone with a smile
Walking down the aisle
I hope they all dance with me too

Look at the beautiful bridesmaid
In thirty years her looks might fade
I'd better be charming
No sleaze - nor alarming
Tradition says I might get laid

My bridesmaids gave me a hen night
Was fine when it started alright
But strippers and shots
Me tied up in knots
Sent to jail when got in a fight!

I'll be the maid of honour - I'm proud
Bride said 'tackiness isn't allowed'
The hens all want madness
Drink, dancing, badness
Shall I be good or break what I vowed?

Best Man

John chose me to be his best man
It's true I'm his number one fan
But I know some stuff
And most of it's rough -
Chapter One - trip in police van

Best man is the important job
Gave it to you, my best friend Rob
We've been friends forever
I hope you'll endeavour
Take care not to let loose your gob

My brother will be my best man
He'll wear a smart suit and spray tan
His speech might be ropey
'Cos he's a bit dopey
With just a short attention span!

What being best man means to me:
Us both standing tall, you and me
Then I'll tell a tale
'Bout you, cops and jail
Then kiss all bridesmaids one, two, three

What's me as Best Man mean to you
Reliable, kind through and through
I've tricks up my sleeve
When the stag party leave
And my speech -you haven't a clue!

Get Well

We're sorry you're poorly, we are
We'll all come to visit by car
Take the pills, eat your greens
So you're soon full of beans
Then we'll go for drinks at the bar

I'm sorry that you're feeling badly
When I heard it made me feel sadly
To get you well soon
I'll sing you a tune
And dance a fast jig for you madly

Hay fever's a pain in the... Nose!
Bad genes? Allergies? I suppose
Steroid spray up your snitch
Wipe your eyes, stop the itch
Pop some pills and pray it soon goes

We know this past week has been hell
Pain, pills and an op since you fell
Your mad extreme sport
Had to be cut short
We know you'll soon mend and get well

We said you look like a baboon
A gentle, endearing lampoon
We hate that you're sick
So get better quick -
I'll see you late this afternoon

Mother's Day & Father's Day

Mothers and Fathers Day

The best dad I know is 'above'
Or reincarnated a dove
He had a few flaws
Was warm, kind (large paws!)
My father taught me how to LOVE

Mother's Day is just commercial ploy
Making money and selling us joy
I don't really care
You're best mum out there
You've loved us all, three girls and a boy

Two days until it's Father's Day
Plans to make it crazy - Wahaay!
Get prezzie and card
Party all night - hard
Then collapse - one more year's decay!

Father, dear Father, why did you leave?
Though I was 5, not too young to grieve
What did I do wrong
That you're gone so long?
Please come back soon - I have to believe...

I love you - today's Father's Day
I love you at work, rest and play
I love you dearest Dad
I love you - such a LAD
"I LOVE YOU," I just want to say

Don't think that we don't appreciate you
We chat more to Mum, 'cos you're quiet too
Your wisdom sustains us
Plus kind fun - with no fuss
For all these great years we'd like to thank you

My mother's a hottie-pa-tottie
Which means she is cute, but quite dotty
As Mum, she's the best
To me and the rest
Have fun, not excess - you'll feel grotty!

You are the very best dad ever
Hold my hand through every endeavour
When I'm bad you don't mind
You're so fair, firm and kind
You love me if I'm dumb or clever

The very best dad that I know
Play football and run, but quite slow
At maths, you're a dope
But try - give me hope
My best friend and I love you so...

New Home

New House

You've bought a new home, what a thrill
You didn't need Kirsty or Phil
Congrats - great endeavour -
You'll live there forever
Or until you're over the hill!

Exciting to have a new house
(A flat that would fit a small mouse!)
Belongs to ME only
But I won't be lonely
With all those mice (if not a spouse)!

We're stoked that you've found your new home
You're settled now - no need to roam
Our house warming present
Is not a dead pheasant
Our gift to you's a garden gnome

Congrats, you've bought a lovely flat
There's room for two kids and a cat
You sure you've got cash?
Not just acting flash?
Can't pay your mortgage - that is that!

You moved to your new house today
Your wise wife has led you astray
You used to squander
And money launder
From now on - steady all the way

New Year

My buddies - a happy New Year
I'm drinking my ninth or tenth beer
My new resolution
Ask for absolution
But for now, I'm just bad I fear

Twenty sixteen will be the best
Most of last year I felt quite stressed
I'm now moving on
From duckling to swan
Cool boyfriend and I've a new nest

Happy New Year to everyone
If it was, we'd shine like the sun
Guess none of us know
How this year will go
We try hard and it may be done...

Unkind words as lay in our beds
What is going on in our heads?
It all starts with drink
Boozed heads cannot think
My heart is broken, torn to shreds

Kind words as we lay in our beds
Bad forgotten, torn into shreds
Love grows, doesn't shrink
'Bout family we think
We're happy, there's joy in our heads

New Baby

New Baby

Congrats, you have a lovely boy
Pain and hard work replaced with joy
You are so clever
He's yours forever
What is his name, Eccles or Troy?

Your little girl was born today. Congratulations!
Yaaay! Hooray!
She's dainty and sweet
Your joy is complete
Together you did it your way...

Your little baby born today
Congratulations! Yaay! Hooray!
He's handsome and neat
Your joy is complete
Together you did it your way...

Baby girl Susan is born hooray!
"Congratulations family," we say
You are so clever
Love her forever
January 12th's the very best day

John and Hayley, couple so sweet
Blessed day they destined to meet
May 5th came Asher
So cute, a smasher
Now fulfilled, their family's complete

Hospital dash, blowing the horn
Mum pushed all through the night till dawn
I just stood around
Drank tea, made no sound
Now I'm a dad, thrilled you've been born

Welcome to the world little one
Big blue eyes that shine like the sun
Be good to your dad
And mum - though they're mad
They'll love you loads, life will be fun

New Job

New Job

You've a fab well paid job - what a thrill!
Though the three interviews made you ill
Forty percent tax!
For now just relax
You'll be minted when 'over the hill'

Well done Tess, you got your new job
At interview - let loose your gob
I bet you looked fit
They thought you were 'it'
I'm sure that you're now their heartthrob

Delighted you got your new job
No longer will you be a slob
Get up every day
Your boss you'll obey
At least you will earn a few bob!

I'm delighted you're now employed
Rude rejections made you annoyed
It went on so long
But you remained strong
We're all really so overjoyed…

Sad

Samaritans there night and day
So tell us your feelings, just say
Suicide or despair
We will listen, we care
Talk - silence – cry. RING ANYWAY

It's good to have a memorial day
For tragedy, worlds disarray
There are thousands unknown
Who are dying alone
Give thought to them, nearby, faraway

'Abide with them, fast falls eventide'
Every day alone and how they've cried
For them life has gone wrong
Just now, or all along
Loving presence, please be at their side

I'm sorry for what I have done
The teasing I did wasn't fun
Think, if I was you
I know what I'd do
I'd put on my trainers and run…

When you came to me, you blue eyed one
Your heart was true, you shone like the sun
When you left again
There's no keener pain
Return to me please, what have we done?

Thanks

I'd like to say thanks to young Ed
He's just built my new flat-packed bed
I'll buy him a beer
Or two, have no fear
And cook tartiflette with fresh bread

Thank you for jump starting my car
Without it I couldn't get far
A horrid wet day
You helped anyway
I'll buy you a drink at the bar

You comfort me with your gentle touch
I fall apart, you're there as my crutch
Love - happy as kings
Laugh at silly things
For our great times, I thank you so much

We went to the beach then watched TV
You showed me the world, helped me to see
We had a few tiffs
But there's no 'what ifs'
Thanks for the great days you gave to me

Kind and helpful - you're a grafter
Cause of all the fun and laughter
Now you have retired
New life, be inspired
We thank you for ever after!

Engagement

Young Lizzie and Rob are engaged
Some women I know are enraged
One wrote a love sonnet
To put a ring on it
But Lizzie's the one got him caged…

We're happy that you're engaged now
She is a gazelle not a cow
You're a bit of a bull
But you managed to pull
We all of us said 'Don't know how…'

He's finally captured your heart
You'll marry - till death do you part
In sickness or health
When poor or with wealth
And bad habits, pick nose or fart

Valentine

Oh John, you're the only one for me
I'll love and treat you so well, you'll see
Please say you are mine
Be my valentine
And happy ever after we'll be

You've loved me since I was sixteen
I thought I was sharp, cool and mean
But now I am fat
And I'm not 'all that'
You still love me as a has-been

You've loved me since I was sixteen
You're stunning and so kind, my queen
Gave girls and a boy
A house full of joy
You're beautiful and still so lean

I drank a toast to you with red wine
Started this morning, just after nine
I'm now off my head
Collapsed in my bed
I guess you won't be my valentine!

Exams

Revision, procrastination
As well as exam frustration
But soon it will end
And your soul will mend
'Cos you'll have summer vacation

You have ten exams - that is tough
And need to revise - you can't bluff
Don't panic, keep calm
You won't come to harm
Holidays will come soon enough

Good luck with your GCSEs
Exams are a stinky disease
But you have worked well
And there's no bad smell
I'm sure it will all be a breeze

My nerves are worse than you'd ever know
Back tomorrow, I don't want to go
Horrid exams next week
Revise like I'm a geek!
Pooing my pants - school I hate you so

Tomorrow is your driving test
Tried before, but this will be best
A smile at the start
Keep calm (and don't fart!)
Concentrate, let skill do the rest...

Retirement

Retirement

Heard through the grapevine you're retired
Time for yourself, you'll be inspired
Or sit and get fat
Smoke, drink, get a cat
Get back to work or you'll be fired!

I'm retired, that makes me feel old
I was given a watch of gold
I'll travel far away
Permanent holiday
Go till I die and turn to mould

Thirty years, you've retired today
No more hassle but no more pay
Now time for some fun
Lie out in the sun
Congratulations, we all say

Retired now, sixty years old
Some fun before death takes its hold
Get a move on mate
It will be too late,
The best advice you have been told

Final day of work, the last one
Be proud of the fine job you've done
And here's the surprise
Golf clubs as your prize
Best employee ever, bar none

Wanted to work till I'm eighty
Pressures of it got too weighty
The boss didn't care
Life just isn't fair
Told him; "Naff off to you, matey"

Random

Random

Today's my first flight on a plane
"I love it," I'm heard to exclaim
"I want to wing-walk
Flap arms like a dork
No wonder they think I'm insane!"

Before...

The marathon's long but you're fit
You've trained hard and got the right kit
Through twenty six miles
Fatigue, pain and smiles
We love you and know you'll do it

After...

The marathon's long but you're fit
You trained hard and had the right kit
Through twenty six miles
Fatigue, pain and smiles
Well done! You're so cool! You did it!

Limericks are my bread and butter
Some are good, some straight from the gutter
Think it's a disease
I caught, just like fleas
I'm itching to tell you, then stutter...

I really want to text my dad
Called 1-1-8, they said; "You're mad!"
He's gone far away
Feels close every day
He's laughing now, I'm not long sad...

Christmas is a time for good cheer
Santa Claus, Rudolf the Reindeer
Give carrots and sherry
So they'll both be merry
And leave a huge sack of gifts here...

Christmas is a family time
Presents, cards and carols that rhyme
With turkey and pud
Love to all men good
Your special day should be sublime

Ramadan, eat night until dawn
Say prayers and recite the Qur'an
Charity, good deeds
Donate the proceeds
Feel joy and delight - not forlorn

I love to observe Divali
Cool clothes, light diyas - I'm Charlie
I go to the States
With family and mates
Puja, mithai - ride a Harley

I love to get stuck in a book
From page 1- my very first look
Perhaps I will frown
If my book's put down
To meet people, go out or cook...

It's a pain when fitted new braces
It hinders then helps people's faces
So please don't be shy
Hold your head up high
If you can't - bend down, tie your laces

How will we know when the world is no more?
Sirens, explosions, house flat to the floor
The body will hurt
Radio divert?
Turn on and there's NO MORE RADIO 4!

My babies all back in the nest
Today for fun, cuddles and jest
Look lovely, they've grown
Work hard, got backbone
But home, act like toddlers regressed...

Goji berries taste yummy and sweet
Like shrivelled cherries squished by your feet!
With antioxidants
(Has seven consonants!)
A superfood which cannot be beat...

I really love Radio 4
World at One, The Archers and more
Just a Minute is best
Graham, Paul and the rest
I hope it thrives for evermore…